THE CLASS PET FROM THE BLACK LAGOON

STORY BY
MIKE THALER

PICTURES BY
JARED LEE

CLASS PET

Cartwheel
·B·O·O·K·S· ®

SCHOLASTIC INC.

New York Toronto London Auckland Sydney
Mexico City New Delhi Hong Kong Buenos Aires

To the wonderful students
at Cherokee Elementary
and to their loving librarian, Michelle Sisk,
and their principal, Mrs. Elizabeth Spurlock.
— M.T.

For Buster, Shane, Brucey, Boots, Ginger, and Spanky...
all dear companions past and present.
— J.L.

ISBN-13: 978-0-545-06930-4
ISBN-10: 0-545-06930-0

Text copyright © 2003 by Mike Thaler.
Illustrations copyright © 2003 by Jared D. Lee Studio, Inc.

20 19 18 17 16 15 14 13 12 11   40   11 12 13 14/0
Printed in the U.S.A. · This edition first printing, September 2008

Mrs. Green is bringing in a class pet.
She won't tell us what it is.

She's bringing it from home—her home!

I wonder what it will look like.
Will it have spots?

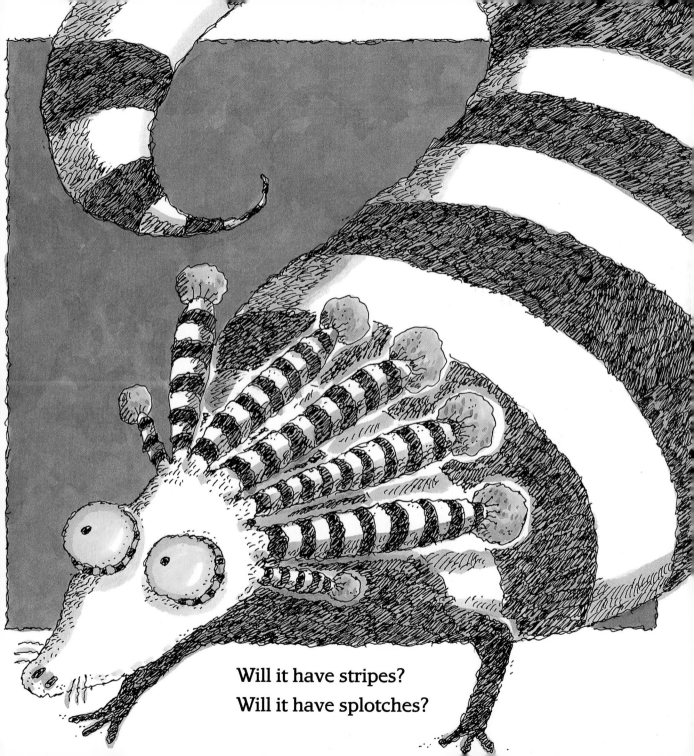

Will it have stripes?
Will it have splotches?

Will it have feathers?

Will it have fur?

Will it have scales?
Will it have horns?

Will it have headlights?

Will it wiggle?

Will it walk?

THUMP
THUMP

Will it hop? Will it jump?

Or will it just sit there like a lump?

Mrs. Green says she's bringing a cage, too!

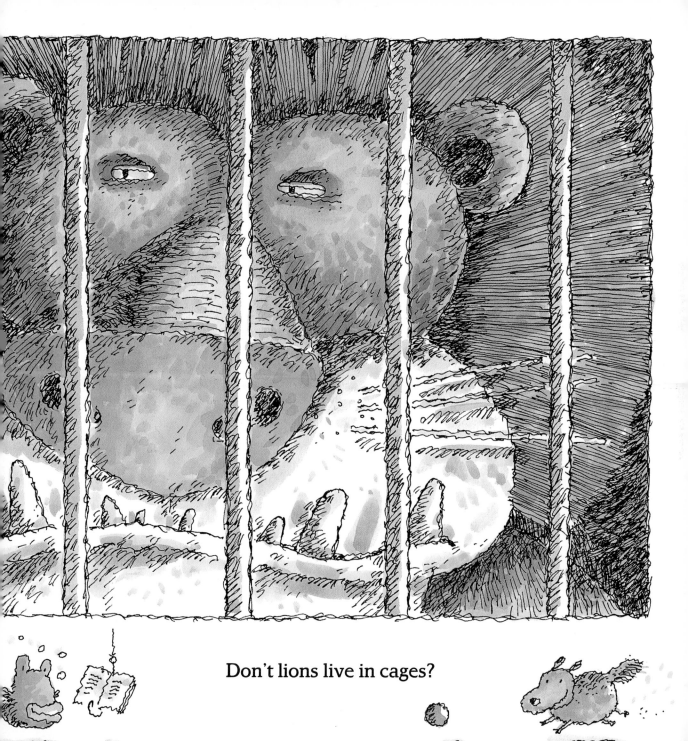

Don't lions live in cages?

Can we pet it?
Can we hold it?

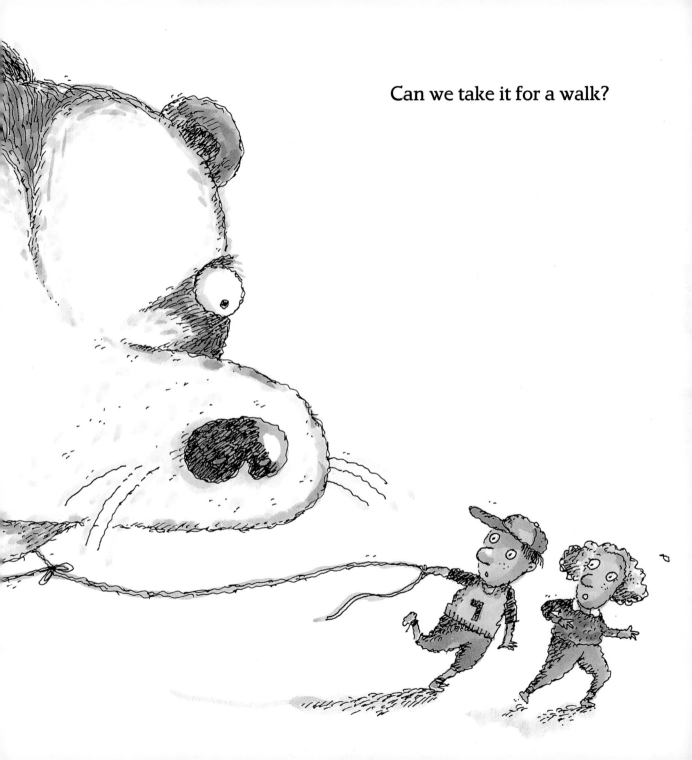

Can we take it for a walk?

And what will it eat? Lettuce? Custard? Us?
Maybe it will be a *carnivore*... and eat cars!

How many legs will it have? And how many teeth?
Two, four, six, eight... what will we appreciate?

Maybe it will be two animals stuck together like a *kangarooster*...

...or a *camelephant*!

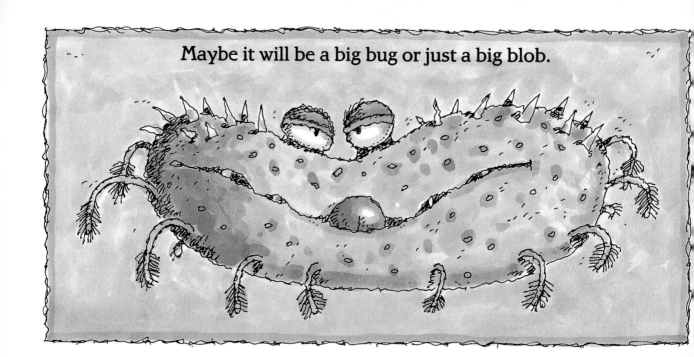

Maybe it will be a big bug or just a big blob.

I'm scared!

Mrs. Green says its first name is Dina.

I hope its last name isn't *Saur*.

Well, here they come.

Two shadows cover the door.

In steps Mrs. Green with a hamster.

It doesn't look too ferocious.
In fact, it looks as scared as we looked.

I'm going to hug it and let it know that it doesn't have anything to be afraid of.